PUFFIN BOOKS

THE PHOENIX AND THE CARPET

'Just say you wish to go abroad.'

So they did, and the next moment there was a whirling, blinding upside-downness, and they were so giddy that they had to shut their eyes.

When they opened them again they were up in the air! The carpet was sailing like a raft in the sky. They peered over the edge and saw sparkling waves and a rocky shoreline.

The Phoenix opened one eye.

'The coast of France,' it said. 'And by the way, I should always keep one wish – for emergencies.'

But the children were not listening.

Some other books by E. Nesbit

THE ENCHANTED CASTLE
FIVE CHILDREN AND IT
THE MAGIC WORLD
THE STORY OF THE TREASURE SEEKERS
NEW TREASURE SEEKERS
THE PHOENIX AND THE CARPET
(*Original version*)
THE RAILWAY CHILDREN
THE STORY OF THE AMULET
THE WOULDBEGOODS

Some other books by Helen Cresswell

LIZZIE DRIPPING
MOONDIAL
ORDINARY JACK
THE PIEMAKERS
THE PUFFIN BOOK OF FUNNY STORIES (Ed.)
THE SECRET WORLD OF POLLY FLINT
THE WATCHERS
STONESTRUCK

For younger readers

DRAGON RIDE
WHATEVER HAPPENED IN WINKLESEA?

The Phoenix and the Carpet

E. Nesbit

Retold by
Helen Cresswell

Based on the BBC TV series

PUFFIN BOOKS

PUFFIN BOOKS

Published by the Penguin Group
Penguin Books Ltd, 27 Wrights Lane, London w8 5tz, England
Penguin Books USA Inc., 375 Hudson Street, New York, New York 10014, USA
Penguin Books Australia Ltd, Ringwood, Victoria, Australia
Penguin Books Canada Ltd, 10 Alcorn Avenue, Toronto, Ontario, Canada m4v 3b2
Penguin Books (NZ) Ltd, 182–190 Wairau Road, Auckland 10, New Zealand

Penguin Books Ltd, Registered Offices: Harmondsworth, Middlesex, England

The Phoenix and the Carpet first published by T. Fisher Unwin, 1904
Published in Puffin Books 1959
Puffin Classic edition published 1994
This retelling first published 1997
1 3 5 7 9 10 8 6 4 2

Text copyright © Helen Cresswell, 1997
A BBC/HIT Entertainment plc Co-production copyright © BBC, 1997
Insert photographs copyright © BBC, 1997
All rights reserved

Puffin Film and TV Tie-in edition first published 1997

The moral right of the author has been asserted

Set in Baskerville
Typeset by Rowland Phototypesetting Ltd,
Bury St Edmunds, Suffolk
Made and printed in England by Clays Ltd, St Ives plc

British Library Cataloguing in Publication Data
A CIP catalogue record for this book is available from the British Library

ISBN 0–140–38976–8

Contents

One
The Egg

NEARLY A HUNDRED years ago there were five children who lived in a tall house in Camden Town, London. Their names, in order of age, were Cyril, Anthea, Robert, Jane and – not forgetting the baby – the Lamb. Then there were mother and father and cook and Eliza, who was the maid.

These children were always having magic adventures. First they met the Psammead, a sand fairy who could grant wishes. They made the most of that – once they were besieged in a castle, and later they flew like birds in the sky! Then they found an amulet that took them all over the world, and back in time.

This particular adventure started on November the Fifth. For days children had been pushing barrows through the streets, yelling, 'Penny for the Guy! Penny for the Guy!'

But our children were to have no bonfire and no fireworks. They were in disgrace. Uncle Felix had given them money to buy fireworks a few days before. And the naughty things had decided to try them out – in the nursery! (I suppose the only excuse was that in those days children did not know how dangerous fireworks are, and that only grown-ups should light them.)

It was a jumping jack that went mad. Cyril tried to put it out with the carpet, but there was lots of fire and smoke, and the carpet was ruined. Cook and Eliza had to whitewash the blackened walls of the nursery, and mother had to buy a new carpet. It wasn't exactly new, but rather threadbare, with a strange pattern.

The first strange thing happened when the carpet was being unrolled. Something flew out and rolled along the bare floor.

'Oh – whatever is it?'

'An egg!' cried Jane. 'It's an egg!'

So it was, but not like any egg they had ever seen before. It was yellow and shiny and had an odd sort of light in it that changed as you held it in different ways. It was as though it had a yoke of pale fire that just showed through the stone.

'We may keep it, mayn't we, mother?' Cyril asked.

Of course, mother said no, they must take it back to Mr Tonks, who had sold her the carpet. It must belong to him.

Luckily, Mr Tonks was not the least bit interested in the egg. So the children put it on the mantelpiece above the fire. From time to time one of them would gaze at it and wonder what it was. But nobody guessed.

On November the Fifth mother and father

went to the theatre. Cook and Eliza were in the basement telling one another's fortunes. Through the window the children could see the glow of bonfires and now and then the whoosh of a rocket.

'Just our luck!' said Robert glumly.

'I wish something would happen!' Jane said. 'Something like the Psammead!'

'I think we're the kind of people magic *does* happen to,' Cyril said. 'And it *would* happen, if we just gave it a shove.'

'Yes, let's!' said Anthea. '*Make* some magic happen!'

They decided to try. They decided that they would make a sacred fire, and dance and chant. (You would have thought they would have learned their lesson!)

They made a sacred fire in the hearth, in front of the real fire. They used pencils made of sweet-smelling sandalwood and eucalyptus oil (for colds) and camphor. They took shawls and scarves from the dressing-up box and began to dance and chant. They swayed and swung their shawls and scarves, and of course

Robert's caught the golden egg, and it fell down inside the fender and rolled under the grate.

'Quick!' screamed Jane. 'Get it out!'

Robert tried to snatch it out but it was already too hot.

'Owch!' he yelled, and the egg flew from his hand and right into the fire.

'Look at it! Look! Look!' cried Anthea. 'I do believe something *is* going to happen!'

For the egg was now red hot, and inside it something was moving. Next moment there was a soft, cracking sound. The egg burst in two, and out of it came a flame-coloured bird. It rested a moment among the flames, and the children could see it growing bigger and bigger under their eyes.

They gaped and goggled.

The bird rose from its nest of fire, stretched its wings and flew out into the room. It flew round and round and round again, and where it passed the air was warm.

Then it perched on the fender. Cyril put out a hand to touch it.

'Be careful!' said the bird. 'I am not nearly cool yet.'

These particular children were not so surprised to hear a bird talk as you or I would have been. They had met magic before, remember.

'Who put my egg in the fire?' the bird asked.

'He did!' said three voices, and three fingers pointed at Robert.

'I am your grateful servant!' it said, and from then on Robert was its favourite.

All the children read lots of books, so they guessed at once that this amazing bird was the Phoenix. It lays an egg, then flies into a fire and is burned up. Then, when it is ready, the egg is put into a fire and the Phoenix hatches out again. And so on and so on.

'I have not been in the world for two thousand years!' it told the children.

'You won't vanish, or do anything sudden, will you?' asked Anthea anxiously.

'Why, do you wish me to stay?'

'Oh yes!' cried four voices.

'You're the most beautiful thing we've ever seen!' added Jane.

The Phoenix preened its golden feathers.

'Then I will not vanish or do anything sudden,' it told them graciously.

'But how did you get here?' asked Robert. 'You don't get Phoenixes in England.'

'Only sparrows and starlings and pigeons,' said Cyril.

So the Phoenix told them how, two thousand years ago, it had laid its egg and placed it on a magic carpet.

'A carpet that gives wishes, that will take you anywhere in the world!'

It told how it had wished the carpet to take the egg somewhere where in two thousand years it would be put on a fire.

'Then I went into the fire and was burned to ashes. And now *you* have burned the egg – and here I am!'

'So – this magic carpet – what was it like?' asked Cyril.

'Oh that,' said the Phoenix carelessly. 'I rather believe it is that one. Yes, I remember the pattern perfectly.'

And it pointed a claw to the floor. It pointed

to the carpet mother had bought from Mr Tonks for twenty-two shillings and ninepence. The children gasped.

At that instant father's latch key was heard in the door.

'*Now* what?' whispered Cyril. 'We shall catch it for not being in bed!'

'Wish yourself there,' said the Phoenix calmly. 'And then wish the carpet back in its place.'

No one knew exactly what happened next, only that it made them rather giddy. Next minute the children were in bed and the lights out.

'Good night!' they heard the Phoenix say in the darkness. 'I shall sleep on the curtain rail.'

'Oh – and we shall see you tomorrow!'

And they all fell asleep, to make tomorrow come more quickly.

Two

The Topless Tower

NEXT DAY WAS Saturday, when mother always took the Lamb to granny's. When she had gone the children planned to try out the magic carpet. As mother was getting ready, Anthea and Jane played the Noah's ark game with the Lamb.

> 'I love my little baby eel
> He is so squidgety to feel.
> He'll be an eel when he is big –
> But now he's just a tiny slig!'

The Lamb was tickled till he wriggled exactly like a real eel. He squealed with delight, and was a baby lion and a baby weasel and a baby rabbit and a baby rat before mother was ready.

Then, at last, the children were alone.

'Better put our hats and coats on,' Cyril said. 'We don't know where we're going.'

Robert gently woke the Phoenix and lifted it on to the carpet, where it went straight back to sleep again. They all sat down and looked at one another. They couldn't decide. Anthea wanted to go to Japan, Robert and Cyril voted for America and Jane for the seaside.

'Not in November, silly!' Cyril told her.

In the end they decided to ask the Phoenix. They woke it up and it murmured drowsily, 'Just say you wish to go abroad.'

So they did, and the next moment there was a whirling, blinding upside-downness, and they were so giddy that they had to shut their eyes.

When they opened them again they were up in the air! The carpet was sailing like a raft in the sky. They peered over the edge and saw sparkling waves and a rocky shoreline.

The Phoenix opened one eye.

'The coast of France,' it said. 'And by the way, I should always keep one wish – for emergencies.'

But the children were not listening. On and on the carpet sailed, and they were so entranced that they forgot about time, until all at once they realized that they were hungry.

'We'll go down and find some grub,' Cyril said.

Then Jane spotted a church tower that looked just the same size as the carpet. She wanted to land on it, but the others told her not to be silly.

'I don't see why I should never do anything I want just because I'm youngest,' she said crossly. 'I wish the carpet would go down to that tower – so there!'

Whoops! The carpet gave a bound and dropped suddenly. Then it was on top of the tower, and then going down and down *inside* it. The tower was hollow.

'Help!' screamed Anthea.

The world was getting darker and the sky above was disappearing.

'Hello – an owl's nest!'

Robert had spotted it, and crawled on to a broad ledge as the carpet went past.

'Look out!' the others yelled.

Down and down the carpet went, leaving Robert behind.

'Jump, you silly cuckoo!'

But it was too late. Next minute three of the children were right at the bottom of the tower, and the other one was stuck on a ledge half-way down.

'Help! Get me down!' Robert's voice echoed in the stony darkness.

'Get off the carpet, quick!' Cyril ordered the girls. They all scrambled off. 'I wish you would go and fetch Robert down!' Cyril commanded.

At once the carpet rose, up and up the tower, and soon it was down again with a very thankful Robert.

'Oh glory!' he gasped. 'That was a squeak!'

'Now what?' Jane asked. 'I'm still hungry!'

'We'll wish to go home,' said Anthea sensibly. 'Then we can have dinner, and this afternoon go somewhere else on the carpet.'

'Not bad, Panther,' Cyril told her. 'Everybody on? Right. I wish we were all safely home!'

They waited for the giddy swirl. Nothing.

'I wish we were all safely home – please,' said Anthea.

Nothing.

'Oh, it hasn't lost its magic, has it? We'll be stuck here for ever and ever!'

Jane was nearly in tears.

'We'd better ask the bird!'

Robert awoke the Phoenix.

'Look here – we wished to be back home, and the carpet hasn't budged!'

'Of course not,' replied the Phoenix. 'I did warn you to keep a wish for emergencies.'

'What do you mean?'

'Why,' said the Phoenix, 'the carpet only gives three wishes a day.'

The children stared at one another in horror.

'And – we've had them!' said Anthea at last.

'Precisely,' nodded the Phoenix.

'So what shall we do?' Jane was crying now.

'I *can* help you, I suppose,' the Phoenix said. 'You won't mind my leaving you for an hour or two?'

Before they could reply, it soared up through the dimness of the tower and into the brightness above.

When it had gone Cyril lit a match and they saw a dark opening in one corner. It led into a deep, dark tunnel, but it might be a way out. Cyril lit one match after another, then, in the darkness between matches, his boot caught against something that made an odd chinking sound. He lit another match and saw that it was an old canvas bag, and spilling out of it were – gold coins.

'Treasure!' shouted Robert. 'Hurray!'

The match went out.

'Light another, quick!'

'That was the last one,' Cyril said.

There was a long, horrid silence. They were trapped in that deep, dark tunnel, and now not even the Phoenix knew where they were.

'Oh!' Jane sobbed. 'I wish we'd never come!'

But the words were no sooner spoken than all the children felt a whirling, and the floor of the cave seemed to lift.

'Earthquake!' Cyril shouted.

But when they opened their eyes they were back in their nursery. There on the mantelpiece sat the Phoenix, looking remarkably pleased with itself.

'Oh clever old Phoenix! How did you do it?'

'Easy,' it told them. 'I just went and asked your friend the Psammead.'

And after that, they counted their wishes very carefully, I can tell you.

Next day, cook gave her notice. It was mainly on account of the children, she said. They had broken her fish slice burying a mouse in the garden, and she had found soap in the suet. And *now* the carpet was covered in nasty yellow mud, though how it had got there goodness alone knew.

The children overheard her telling tales to mother.

'Cantankerous cat!' said Robert.

'Beastly blue-nosed Bozwoz!' agreed Cyril.

They didn't mind seeing the back of cook, but were sorry that her going upset mother, who was worried enough already about the Lamb's cough.

'I know!' said Jane. 'As soon as mother's gone out this afternoon, we'll make another wish and take the Lamb with us! Somewhere nice and sunny that will do his cough good.'

No one had seen the Phoenix since yesterday. It seemed to need a lot of sleep, for someone who had already been asleep for two thousand years.

'Well, I know it hasn't deserted us,' said Robert. 'It's a bird of its word.'

'Quite so!' said a voice.

It was the Phoenix. It had been there all

the time, perched on a bar under the table, hidden by the cloth. It told them that if people wanted to call it, they usually had to chant something called an Ode of Invocation. It was seven thousand lines long, and written in pure Greek. In the end, it agreed that it would let the children off. In future, if they wanted to call it, they must chant, 'Oh come along, good old beautiful Phoenix, come along, come along!'

So the children crowded on to the carpet with the Phoenix and were ready to go when the door burst open. There was cook, waving a broken basin.

'Look 'ere!' she screeched. ''ow in the name of 'eaven am I to make the steak and kidney pudding your ma ordered for your dinners?'

'I'm awfully sorry, cook,' said Anthea.

'And my gracious cats alive! What've you got that blessed baby dressed up in his out-doors for?'

'Look here,' said Cyril. 'Can't you go and make your steak and kidney in a flowerpot or something?'

'Not me!' said cook.

Then the Phoenix spoke up.

'I warn you!' it said sternly. 'Beware, before it is too late!'

The cook stared. Her eyes popped.

'Wherever did you get that there yellow fowl?'

The Phoenix drew itself up and glared. The Lamb began to howl. The children were desperate.

'I wish – I wish we were on a sunny southern shore where there aren't any coughs!' cried Anthea.

She had not noticed that cook was on the carpet, too. Next minute they all had that giddy, whirling topsy-turvy feeling and the floor tilted and cook shrieked and – whoosh!

When they opened their eyes they were a thousand miles away from foggy Camden Town. The hot sun beat down on white sands and a pure blue sea. Palm trees waved.

'I say!' Cyril looked round and whistled.

All four of them started to peel off their

coats and hats, and Anthea pulled off the Lamb's boots.

'There!' she said. 'Can you feel your little piggy toes in the sand?'

As for cook, she opened her eyes, shrieked, and shut them again. Open. Shriek. Shut. Open. Shriek.

'It's a dream!' she said at last. 'I'm in a dream! Well, it's the best I've ever dreamed!'

And she just sat there, a happy, vacant smile on her face, and looked as if she would sit there for ever. But the children wanted to explore, so they left her there. Off they went, the Lamb riding piggyback on Cyril's back, and the Phoenix perched on Robert's wrist.

Three

The Queen Cook

T HE ISLAND WAS magical. Under the trees there were tangled creepers with bright, strange-shaped flowers. Scarlet blossom hung from the boughs and brilliant birds darted about quite close to their faces. The children followed a path that turned and twisted, then stopped to let the Lamb pick flowers. And all the time he had not coughed once.

Then they heard the sound of strange music, far off. They were not alone on the island.

'Savages!' gasped Anthea.

'Cannibals!' shrieked Jane. 'Oh, suppose they eat us!'

They turned and ran, back through the trees and on to the wide, sandy shore. But there, at a little distance, was a group of natives, all singing and playing strange instruments, and marching towards them.

'Back to the carpet!' Cyril ordered. 'Quick!'

'*I* will talk to them,' said the Phoenix. 'I am not afraid.'

The children raced back to where they had left cook. They stopped and stared in horror. There was the pile of their hats and coats – but cook had vanished – and the carpet!

The sound of music and shouting was louder now, and they saw that the natives had nearly reached them.

'Look!' said Cyril. 'What are they pointing at?'

'Something in the sea,' said Robert.

They turned. There, bobbing among the waves, was the white hat of the cook. Robert started to splash towards her.

'What on earth did you come out here for?' he shouted. 'And where on earth's the carpet?'

'It's not on earth, bless you,' replied cook happily. 'It's under me, in the water! I got a bit warm sitting in the sun, and I just says, "I wish I was in a cold bath!" – just like that! And next minute, here I was!'

'Oh no!' groaned Cyril. 'She's used another wish!'

Now there was only one left, and for all the children knew they were among cannibals.

'Excuse me,' said the Phoenix's voice. 'These people want your cook.'

'What – to eat?' gasped Jane in horror.

'Not to eat,' replied the Phoenix. 'As their queen.'

It had been talking to the natives in their own language. That was easy, it said, all part of the carpet's magic. And it seemed there was an ancient story that said one day a queen would come to them out of the sea and wearing a white crown.

'Cook's hat!'

'Exactly,' nodded the Phoenix.

Cook was helped out of the sea, and the people all surrounded her. They bowed and curtsied and garlanded her with flowers. The boys hauled the carpet ashore, dripping wet now and caked with sand.

Cook was pleased as Punch with what she thought was her dream. She smiled graciously and held out her fat red hands to be kissed.

'Well, *I'm* certainly not kissing them!' said Robert in disgust. 'Let's go home!'

'Oh but we can't go and leave poor cook!' said Anthea.

But cook wanted to stay. She would have a far better life here than in Camden Town, cooking day after day in a dark basement.

So the children crowded on to the soggy carpet, and the Phoenix fluttered to Robert's wrist, and they wished to be home.

Next minute they were. But they had hardly tumbled off the carpet when the nursery door burst open and there was Eliza.

'She's gone!' she shrieked. 'Cook's gone!'

Of course, mother was upset at losing cook, and Anthea still thought it was mean of them to have left cook alone on the island so far away from home. So she got up early next morning and sat on the carpet and wished to be back on the sunny southern shore. She need not have worried. Cook had been crowned queen and was waited on hand and foot, and had not the least wish to be back home.

So that was all right.

It was Eliza who found a new cook. Her name was Lily, and she was Eliza's sister-in-law.

'It's a bit funny, the other cook going off like that,' she told Eliza, as the pair of them sat in the kitchen drinking tea and eating caraway seed cake.

'It's them children,' Eliza told her.

'What? Fussy about their food, are they?'

'Oh lawks no!' said Eliza. 'You just keep giving 'em mutton stew and semolina, they'll never starve. The missis is taking the Lamb to Bournemouth and the master's off to Scotland, so you and me'll have a nice easy time of it.'

*

Once their parents had left, and the Lamb, the house seemed very quiet. The children looked for the Phoenix, but could not find it anywhere.

'I know what,' said Anthea. 'Let's go on the carpet to Bournemouth and see mother and the Lamb!'

'Oh yes!' cried Jane. 'But – won't she wonder how on earth we got there?'

They thought hard.

'I know,' said Cyril. 'We'll wish for us to be able to see her, but for her not to be able to see us.'

So they sat on the carpet and wished. Next minute they opened their eyes and found themselves in a sandy cove. There, seated under the pine trees, was mother, reading a book. The Lamb was playing happily near by. They were so close that the children could hardly believe that if mother looked up from her book she would not see them.

The Lamb soon spotted them. He dropped his bucket and spade and toddled towards them, trying to say their names in his funny, mixed-up way. He called Anthea Panty, Jane Pussy, Cyril Squiggle and Robert Bobs. He talked a language of his own that the other children called Bosh.

Anthea and Jane picked him up and kissed him, and the boys thumped their little brother on his back. Then Anthea put him on her knee and played the Noah's ark game.

'I love my little baby bear,
I love his nose and toes and hair;
I like to hold him in my arm,
And keep him very safe and warm.'

Of course the Lamb wriggled and gurgled and squealed and then mother did look up. She turned quite pale. There was her darling Lamb, squirming and chuckling in mid-air, or so it seemed. She dropped her book and hurried over so quickly that the children had to jump back or she would have run into them. She snatched up the Lamb and looked about her. It seemed impossible that she could not see Anthea, Cyril, Robert and Jane. And she looked so frightened that they wished like

Mother had to buy a new carpet. It wasn't exactly new, but rather thread-bare, with a strange pattern.

(Ian Keith as father, Mary Waterhouse as mother, Freddie Ward as the Lamb, and Christopher Biggins as Mr Tonks – Photographer: Joss Barratt)

The children guessed at once that this amazing bird was the Phoenix.

(Ivan Berry as Robert, Jessica Fox as Anthea, Charlotte Chinn as Jane, and Ben Simpson as Cyril – Photographer: Joss Barratt)

When the children opened their eyes they were a thousand miles away from foggy Camden Town.

(Ben Simpson as Cyril, Jessica Fox as Anthea, Charlotte Chinn as Jane, and Ivan Berry as Robert – Photographer: Joss Barratt)

Cook wanted to stay. She would have a far better life on the island than in Camden Town.

(Miriam Margolyes as cook, IROKO with supporting artists as the islanders – Photographer: Joss Barratt)

Cyril told the Ranee the story of the carpet, and how it had brought them the Phoenix.

(Ivan Berry as Robert, Charlotte Chinn as Jane, Jessica Fox as Anthea, Ben Simpson as Cyril, Zina Badran as an Indian lady, and Kim Vithana as the Ranee – Photographer: Joss Barratt)

Cyril explained how they had come to India in search of things for his mother's stall.

(Ivan Berry as Robert, Charlotte Chinn as Jane, Jessica Fox as Anthea, Ben Simpson as Cyril, Zina Badran as an Indian lady, Kim Vithana as the Ranee – Photographer: Joss Barratt)

The tablecloth was whisked up and there, towering above them, was a very cross-looking lady.

(Ivan Berry as Robert, Charlotte Chinn as Jane, Jessica Fox as Anthea, and Ben Simpson as Cyril – Photographer: Joss Barratt)

Robert scrambled out, followed by Cyril. Mrs Biddle stared and glowered.

(Gemma Jones as Mrs Biddle – Photographer: Joss Barratt)

Anthea tried to explain as politely as she could that they had brought things for mother's stall.

(Ivan Berry as Robert, Charlotte Chinn as Jane, Ben Simpson as Cyril, and Jessica Fox as Anthea – Photographer: Joss Barratt)

The argument went on and on.

(Mark Powley as Uncle Felix, Gemma Jones as Mrs Biddle, and Miranda Pleasence as Miss Peasmarsh – Photographer: Joss Barratt)

Uncle Felix offered to help Miss Peasmarsh sell the Indian trinkets.

(Mark Powley as Uncle Felix, and Miranda Pleasence as Miss Peasmarsh – Photographer: Joss Barratt)

As they approached the covered market, some ragged children appeared.

(Jamie Sweeney as carol singer – Photographer: Joss Barratt)

The burglar saw an amazing sight. Cook was sitting and singing, crowned with flowers and surrounded by attendants.

(Miriam Margolyes as cook, and Shaun Dingwall as the burglar – Photographer: Chris Capstick)

The burglar was not in the least surprised to see the children on the island.

(Shaun Dingwall as the burglar, Ivan Berry as Robert, Charlotte Chinn as Jane, Ben Simpson as Cyril, and Jessica Fox as Anthea – Photographer: Chris Capstick)

They were getting on so well that the burglar asked cook to marry him.

(Shaun Dingwall as the burglar, and Miriam Margolyes as cook – Photographer: Chris Capstick)

At the end of the first act, an attendant came to ask the children to keep their bird quiet.

(The Phoenix – Photographer: Joss Barratt)

anything that they had never come. She hurried off, looking over her shoulder.

'*That* didn't go off very well,' said Cyril miserably at last.

'Oh it was horrible! She looked right through us!' cried Jane. 'Let's go home! Oh please, let's go home!'

Four
Two Bazaars

T HE CHILDREN WERE upset about frightening their mother. They tried to think of something they could do to please her, and make up for it. Anthea remembered that mother had been going to help with the Christmas bazaar on Saturday. She had been meaning to find lots of exciting things for her stall.

'So let's wish to go somewhere where people will give us things for the stall!'

'Oh yes! Brass and bangles and shawls and things!' said Jane.

'Then we can take them straight to the bazaar and sell them,' said Cyril.

So when Saturday came they all crowded on to the carpet. This time they did not wear their outdoor things (though later they would wish they had). Again they could not find the Phoenix, and supposed it must be having another of its naps.

'I've never known a bird sleep so much as that one,' said Cyril – as if he had known hundreds of birds, which he certainly had not.

So they made the wish and, after the usual blinding, tumbling, whirling upside-downness, found themselves again in hot sunlight. They were right in the middle of a busy bazaar, and guessed at once that they were in India.

A man went by on an elephant and near by was a snake-charmer. There, all around them, were the shining brassware and silken shawls, exactly as they had hoped.

'It's no go, though,' Cyril said.

The others looked at him.

'We wished for people to *give* us things. These people are poor and can't afford to.'

But the carpet's magic was working. Two ladies appeared, dressed in silk trousers and veils. They smiled and greeted the children. Their mistress, the Ranee (an Indian queen), had seen them from her palace, and wished to speak to them.

'Rather!' said Robert. 'A palace!'

The Ranee sat on silken cushions and she was decorated with gold and jewels. Two turbaned men fanned her with peacock feathers. The children bowed and curtsied, rather overawed by the splendour.

The Ranee pointed to the rolled-up carpet under Cyril's arm.

'Do you wish to sell it?' she asked.

'No!' answered four voices at once.

'Why?' she asked.

Cyril told her. He told her the story of the carpet, and how it had brought them the Phoenix. Then he told of the adventure in France, and how cook had gone with them to the South Sea island.

'And she's still there, and she's queen!' he ended.

The Ranee laughed and clapped and all her court followed suit.

'You are a heaven-born teller of tales!' she told Cyril. She took a string of turquoises from her neck and tossed them to him.

'How lovely!' gasped Anthea and Jane, but Cyril shook his head.

He explained how they had come to India in search of things for his mother's stall, but that precious jewels were far too valuable. So the Ranee asked the children to tell her another story, and then she would send to the bazaar for pretty things.

Anthea told the story of the Psammead, and how it granted their wishes. The Ranee loved it every bit as much as the first. She clapped her hands, and the servants brought trays of delicious food. While the children ate it, men went to the bazaar and fetched trays full of pretty things and piled them on to the carpet.

Then the children thanked the Ranee and got on to the carpet.

'I wish we were at mother's bazaar in Camden Town!' said Cyril.

And of course, next minute they were. Luckily the thoughtful carpet dumped the children and their treasures in a dim corner, where no one would notice. Robert, still dizzy, started to crawl under a table, but as he did so a large, heavy boot came down smack on his hand.

'Oooooowch!'

At once the tablecloth was whisked up and there, towering above him, was a very cross-looking lady. It was Mrs Biddle, who was organizing the bazaar. Behind her were the Reverend Septimus Blenkinsop and his two sisters, Selina and Amelia.

'Are you all right, Bobs?' called Anthea anxiously.

'That *hurt*!' said Robert.

'Oh I'm sorry, I'm sure!' said Mrs Biddle huffily. 'I do beg your pardon!'

Robert scrambled out, followed by Cyril. Mrs Biddle stared and glowered.

'Whatever do you mean by creeping about under stalls like earwigs!' she demanded.

The two girls came out, and Anthea tried

to explain as politely as she could that they had brought things for mother's stall.

'Except that she's not here,' said Cyril. 'So perhaps someone else could sell them for her?'

'I should like to see them, if I may,' said pretty Miss Peasmarsh, on the next stall. 'I haven't much to sell, I'm afraid.'

But by then Anthea had brought out a tray crammed with beautiful brassware and sandalwood boxes. Mrs Biddle's eyes stretched.

'Excuse *me*,' she said. 'Those objects were behind *my* stall. I expect they were sent to me by an unknown admirer.'

'Fat chance!' muttered Cyril.

Then Uncle Felix, who had promised mother he would attend, appeared. He took one look at the pretty Miss Peasmarsh and was on her side.

'Oh Uncle Felix!' cried Anthea. 'We've brought all this Indian stuff for mother, and –'

'– and that horrid Mrs Biddle says they're *hers*!' finished Jane.

'Now, now,' murmured the Reverend Septimus Blenkinsop. 'Peace, ladies, peace!'

The argument went on and on. But Anthea went back under the stall and wrote a note. It said 'All these things are for nice pretty Miss Peasmarsh's stall'. She put it on a tray of trinkets and brought it out.

When Mrs Biddle saw it she was furious, and said that it looked like the work of a lunatic. But the Indian things went on to Miss Peasmarsh's stall, and Uncle Felix offered to help her sell them.

'I think he's sweet on her!' whispered Jane to Anthea. They both giggled, while their brothers frowned at such soppiness.

By now the children had forgotten that Eliza and Lily would be expecting them home. Uncle Felix slipped them half a crown, and they went on all the side-shows – the bran tub and fishing for goldfish.

Much later, they spotted Uncle Felix having tea with Miss Peasmarsh, and went to join them. Uncle Felix said they could have as many cream cakes as they could eat. He was in a very good mood, and so was Miss Peasmarsh.

'We've sold every single thing!' said Uncle Felix. 'Every last dicky bird!'

'Er – the carpet . . .' began Cyril. 'We have to –'

'Oh – I've even sold that!' cried Miss Peasmarsh gaily.

The children froze.

'To Mrs Biddle! She gave me ten shillings for it!'

Five

Mrs Biddle
Transmogrified

MISS PEASMARSH WAS puzzled by the children's horrified faces.

'I'm sorry – did I do wrong?'

Anthea explained that it was their own carpet, from home. They had just used it to put the things on.

'Come on,' said Cyril. 'We've got to do something!'

Their first idea was to buy the carpet back. They counted their money and found that they had twelve shillings and threepence.

'I'll ask her,' said Cyril. 'I'm eldest, and I've got the best manners.'

He marched over to where Mrs Biddle still had a stall full of ugly and useless things to sell.

'Er . . . excuse me . . .' he began.

'What?' snapped Mrs Biddle.

'It's about that carpet.' He pointed to where it lay rolled up by the stall. 'It's ours, you see.'

'Yours?' cried Mrs Biddle. 'Whatever do you mean? I bought it not ten minutes ago for ten shillings. It's mine.'

'Yes,' said poor Cyril. 'But – would you sell it to us? We'd give you all –'

He held out his hand with the money in it.

'Certainly not!' said Mrs Biddle. 'Go away, little boy! Go away!'

Cyril went back to the others and they all had another think. They came up with the idea that Jane should pretend to be a fortune-teller with a crystal ball. She would then warn

37

Mrs Biddle about a carpet that had an ancient curse laid on it, and brought bad luck to whoever owned it.

She draped a shawl over her head, and Anthea borrowed a large glass paperweight from a nearby stall. Cyril wrote a notice saying: 'Madame Slavinsky. Crystal Ball. Two pence.'

Then Anthea went to Mrs Biddle and offered to look after the stall while she went round the rest of the bazaar.

'There's a simply wonderful fortune-teller!' she said cunningly.

'Hmph! Superstitious nonsense!' sniffed Mrs Biddle.

All the same she went off, and the first thing she did was take her place at the table where Jane sat staring at the crystal ball till her eyes watered.

'The mists are clearing . . .' Jane crooned, in what she hoped was a singsong voice. 'I see . . . oooh . . . I see a dire and doomy thing . . .'

'A what?' demanded Mrs Biddle.

'Doom . . . an ancient curse . . . I see a

carpet . . . yes, an old magic carpet from the ancient land of Persia . . . ooh . . . and it brings ill luck to whoever walks on it . . .'

Mrs Biddle leapt up and snatched the shawl from Jane's head.

'Madame Slavinsky indeed!' she cried. 'Crystal ball!' And she flounced back to her stall.

'We'll *burgle* it back!' said Robert.

First they had to find out where Mrs Biddle lived. By the time they saw the cab set down Mrs Biddle and the carpet at her house, it was nearly dark.

'We'd better wait and do the burgling tomorrow,' Cyril said. 'Eliza will be in a fearful wax!'

And so she was.

'You wicked, wicked children! Out all hours, and without your coats and 'ats! Bed, this very minute, the lot of you!'

Next day the children had to think of ways to stop Eliza coming up to the nursery. If she did, she might notice that the carpet was missing. So Jane and Anthea went and offered to carry all the trays upstairs. Meantime, the boys thought up another plan.

'Totters!' said Robert.

These were people who went from house to house, buying and selling old things.

'We'll dress up, and use the Lamb's pram as a barrow!'

'But what if Mrs Biddle recognizes us?'

'Totters don't go round to *front* doors, pudding head! They talk to maids and such!'

So Cyril and Robert piled the Lamb's pram high with battered saucepans and cushions. They smeared their faces with grime and wore raggedy clothes. They had to wait till Eliza and Lily were having their Sunday afternoon snooze before they could go.

'Where's that Phoenix?' said Cyril. 'No carpet, and no Phoenix!'

'I hope it hasn't bunked off for good,' said Robert.

They searched high and low but there was not a sign of it.

As soon as dinner was over the boys sneaked out and made for Mrs Biddle's house. The back door was opened by the maid, Grace. She stared at the two ragged and grubby boys and their pram.

'Not today, thank you!' she said, and started to close the door.

'Wait! We're not selling – we're buying!' said Cyril.

'Any old rubbish,' added Robert. 'Especially old carpets.'

'Oooh, funny, you should say that!!' said Grace. 'The missis – she came home only yesterday with this horrible old carpet!'

'We'll take it!' said Cyril.

'Five bob sight unseen!' said Robert.

Just then came a loud, familiar voice.

'Grace! Grace! Who is it?'

Next minute the door was banged shut in their faces. The trick had failed.

'So that leaves burglaring!' said Robert.

They waited till it was nearly dark, and set out again, all four of them, for Mrs Biddle's house. They stood nervously looking at it. Nobody really wanted to be a burglar, except perhaps Robert.

'I think we should give her one last chance,' said Anthea.

'You could cry, Jane,' Robert told her. 'You can turn the waterworks on and off like a tap.'

They knocked, and the minute Grace opened the door they went straight past her into the house, and into the room where they could see Mrs Biddle. They could see their precious carpet, too. She was standing on it.

'You!' she cried. 'You wicked daring little things! How dare you!'

'Please don't be angry,' wailed Jane, and she sniffed and gulped, trying to work herself up to tears.

'Please let us have our carpet back,' begged Anthea.

'Grace – show them out this minute!'

'We're offering to buy it back,' said Cyril desperately.

'Giving you a last chance,' said Robert.

Mrs Biddle was scarlet with fury.

'How dare you! How dare you!'

Jane gave up trying to cry, and marched straight up to her.

'You look perfectly horrid!' she said loudly.

'You rude, barefaced child!'

'It really *is* our carpet – you just ask anyone if it isn't!'

'Grace – call the police!'

The maid hurried from the room.

'Let's just get on the carpet and wish ourselves home!' whispered Cyril to Robert.

'What – with *her*?'

Cyril looked down and saw Mrs Biddle's boots planted firmly on the carpet.

Anthea had an inspiration. She stepped just on to the carpet and said 'Oh – I do wish Mrs Biddle was in an angelic good temper!'

For an instant Mrs Biddle's face froze. Then it melted into an amazing, radiant beam. She was transmogrified.

'Why!' she cried. 'Why shouldn't I be in a good temper, my dears?'

'You're a jolly good sort, Mrs Biddle,' said Robert.

'Dear little boy! And I trod on your poor hand! I'm so sorry!'

'And we're sorry we annoyed you at the bazaar,' said Cyril.

'Not another word!' said Mrs Biddle. 'Of course you shall have the carpet, my dears. It is, now I look at it, a very *ordinary* carpet.'

Jane put a hand over her mouth to hide a smile.

'Thank you! Thank you very much!' said Anthea.

'Not at all. I'm delighted to be able to give any little pleasure to such dear children. Such dear, dear children!'

She beamed, and the children beamed back. Cyril and Robert stooped to roll up the carpet.

'Don't hurry off! Stay and have some mince pies! Grace! Grace!'

So the children stayed. They had first mince pies, then trifle, and forgot all about the time, and Eliza and Lily.

When they got home they went in quietly, on tiptoe. But Robert tripped and knocked an umbrella from the stand with a clatter. Next minute Eliza and Lily were there.

44

'And what bazaar you been to *this* time of a Sunday?' demanded Eliza. 'And what's that you've got there?'

She had spotted the carpet, which Robert and Cyril were trying vainly to hide.

'What've you been doing walking round with a carpet?' asked Lily.

'There's no wonder it gets mud on it!' shrieked Eliza. 'Here – *I'll* 'ave that carpet!'

She seized it, but Cyril and Robert would not let go. There was a fierce tug of war, which ended by the boys suddenly giving up and Eliza falling back against the hat stand.

'Off to bed!' she screeched. 'Off to bed!'

Without a word the children went up the stairs. Eliza and Lily stood shaking their heads.

'Roaming round London without their 'ats and coats,' said Eliza, as if saying it aloud would make it more believable. 'In the dark. With a *carpet*.'

Six
Kidnapped

ELIZA LOCKED THE carpet in the cupboard under the stairs. The children couldn't find the Phoenix, either, though they searched for days. It began to look as if their wonderful adventures had come to an end. Then Robert remembered.

'The invocation!'

They had clean forgotten.

'Here goes!' said Robert. 'All together! Oh come along, come along, you good old beautiful Phoenix!'

They waited.

'Again!' said Robert.

'Oh come along, come along, you good old beautiful Phoenix!'

There was a rustling, and the Phoenix sailed into the room on wide gold wings. The children cheered.

'Where on earth have you been?' demanded Robert. 'We've been looking for you everywhere.'

'And I might have come out if I had heard my invocation,' the Phoenix replied. 'Where is the magic carpet?'

Of course, they had to confess. To their surprise, the Phoenix did not seem to mind very much. It said they would lose the use of their legs if they went everywhere by carpet.

'I wish to see London,' it announced.

So the girls put on their best scarlet hats and coats in honour of the Phoenix, and they set off, Robert carrying the Phoenix in a bag.

'This isn't much of an outing!' came the

Phoenix's muffled voice. 'I can't see a thing!'

As they approached the covered market, three ragged children appeared.

'Ooh look!' squealed the girl. 'Little dukes and ladies!'

'Lah di dah! Lah di dah!' mocked the bigger boy, and, 'Oooh, Santa's little 'elpers!' jeered the other.

'Rude things!' said Jane.

'It's your fault,' Robert told the girls. 'Coming out in those flashy coats!'

'Quick – in here!' Cyril darted up the wide stone steps to the market and the others hurried after him.

The stalls were piled with glowing mounds of fruit and nuts and all kinds of things for Christmas. Near by a fiddler was scraping out carols.

'Oh, isn't it pretty!' said Jane.

'I can't see!' came the Phoenix's cross voice. 'I think you are forgetting that this is my outing!'

'Lah di dah! Nah then, you four little girls, 'ow's tricks?'

'I'll little girl you!' Robert was furious. He dropped the bag and put up his fists.

'That's it!' cried one boy. 'Give it to 'im, Ike!' And he snatched Robert's cap from his head. The girls screamed, and the pair began to fight. Nobody noticed the little ragged girl pick up the bag and run off.

Robert and Ike biffed and punched till they were breathless. Then Ike, with a final swipe, yelled, 'There's a last one for a Merry Christmas! Beat it, Erb!'

The pair raced off, Erb tossing Robert's cap into the air and catching it as he ran. Robert and Cyril gave chase, and it was only then that . . .

'The bag!' screamed Jane, looking round. 'That girl! That beastly girl!'

They too started to run. Meantime, Erb and Ike, who knew the market like the back of their hands, ducked and dived between stalls and pillars, and disappeared. Robert and Cyril stood panting.

'My cap!' gasped Robert. 'Eliza'll throw a fit!'

Then the girls were there.

'The Phoenix!' cried Jane. 'We've got to get it back!'

The chase was on again. At last, when they had almost given up, Cyril spotted the three, sitting on some nearby steps. Rose was just opening the bag.

'Eeech!' she screamed. 'It's alive!'

Erb and Ike peered cautiously in.

'It's a fowl!' exclaimed Erb. 'A great yeller fowl!'

'Wring its neck!' said Ike.

''Ave it stuffed wiv sage and onion for Christmas!' said Erb. He was wearing Robert's cap.

The four children crept forward and surrounded the trio.

'Oooh!' said Erb. 'If it ain't them little girls again!'

'Give us the bag!' said Cyril sternly. 'It's ours.'

'Oh no you don't!' Ike whipped up the bag and held it behind his back.

'Oh don't hurt it, please!' begged Jane.

'Tell you what,' said Erb. 'Give us a quid, and it's yours!'

He grabbed the bag and dangled it above his head.

But the children didn't have any money.

'Do stop swinging me so!' came the muffled voice of the Phoenix.

The three urchins goggled.

'It's talking!'

'A parrot! A yeller parrot!'

'Worth a fortune!'

''Ere – catch!'

Erb tossed Robert's cap high into the air. As all four children ran forward to catch it, the other three were off in a flash. Within seconds they were gone. And so was the Phoenix.

They searched high and low, but in the end they had to go home.

'Oh now what, now what?' sobbed Jane. 'We'll never see it again!'

The others knew that this might be true. London is a big place, and by now the Phoenix could be anywhere.

When they got home there was a letter from mother. They were all to spend Christmas in Bournemouth, for a whole week, up to New Year.

'But it won't be a Christmassy Christmas at all without the Phoenix,' said Anthea sadly.

'And I won't be able to eat a single mouthful of Christmas dinner,' said Jane.

The others knew what she meant. They remembered what Erb had said about sage and onion stuffing.

Straight after dinner they went out to search again for their beloved Phoenix. They went to the market, but there was not a sign. Further and further they went, further from home than they had ever been before. Nothing.

Finally they turned and began to drag their feet wearily towards home. As they passed Mr Tonks's shop, Cyril had an idea.

'I know! That's where it came from remember!'

Mr Tonks came out from the back of the shop.

'I say,' began Cyril, 'you haven't by any chance seen –'

'– an egg!' said Anthea. 'A beautiful golden egg!'

'Like the one that came rolled up in the carpet,' added Robert.

'Or a bird,' said Cyril. 'A big golden bird?'

'*Bird?*' said Mr Tonks. 'In a *carpet?*'

Then Jane shrieked.

'Here! Oh here!'

She had been looking in through the window of the pet shop next door. Now she rushed inside, followed by the others. It was dim and crowded and the air was filled with the cheep of birds. There among them, hanging in a large cage, was the Phoenix. Its head drooped and its eyes were closed.

'Hurray!' shouted the boys.

'Oh Phoenix!' cried Jane. 'Darling Phoenix, wake up!'

The owner came scurrying out from the back of the shop.

''Ere! What's all the row? Ah. My prize bird!'

'It's the Phoenix!' said Anthea.

'New in today,' he told them. 'What a beauty! What a specimen!'

'Oh why doesn't it open its eyes?' wailed Jane.

'Ho, you don't want to worry about that, miss,' the owner told her. 'It ain't dead. Oh no. Talks!'

The children exchanged glances.

'We want to buy it,' said Cyril.

'What? You are a joking. You are a-having me on!'

'No, we really do want it!' said Anthea.

'Oh I don't think you'll run to the bird. Ho no. Not unless you've come into a fortune, or your pa's a duke.'

'Why, how much is it?'

'Twenty guineas!' he said. The children gasped, horror-struck. 'Cage hincluded.'

It seemed like the end of the world. The children went home and counted their money, but had barely one guinea, let alone twenty.

'Hopeless,' said Cyril. 'It's hopeless.'

'The invocation!' said Robert suddenly.

It was worth a try. They chorused together, 'Oh come along, come along, you good old beautiful Phoenix!'

They chanted it twenty times, but there was no rustle of wide golden wings.

There were only a few days left before Christmas, and they tried as hard as they could to raise the money. Cyril made a collection in the street: SAVE THE BIRDS. The girls tried to pawn their best dolls. Robert set up on a street corner, busking with his mouth organ.

Every single day they went to visit the Phoenix in the pet shop. Every time it was hunched in its cage, its eyes shut. But at least it was still there.

'Still plenty of time for someone to buy it as a Christmas present,' said Cyril glumly.

The night before they were to leave for Bournemouth the children huddled round the nursery fire where first they had seen the Phoenix.

'Come along, oh come along, you good old beautiful Phoenix!'

They gave up in the end, and gazed sadly into the flames.

'It's our fault,' said Anthea at last. 'It's all our fault.'

'I know,' agreed Cyril miserably.

Jane was crying.

'It won't be a Christmassy Christmas at all,' she sobbed.

'That old bird was magic,' said Robert gruffly.

'Oh dear old Phoenix,' whispered Anthea, 'if you can hear us . . . we're sorry . . . we're dreadfully, dreadfully sorry . . .'

Seven
Mews from Persia

JANE WAS RIGHT. Christmas just wasn't the same. Of course they enjoyed the presents and the food, but all the time the children were thinking of the Phoenix, all alone in that dark corner, or worse still – sold.

Before they left Bournemouth they went to visit their old friend the Psammead, who lived in a sandpit near by. When they had last seen it they had promised they would not ask for any more wishes. But this, they told themselves, was an emergency.

'The Psammead has a heart of gold, even if it does get cross sometimes,' Jane said.

And so it turned out. The Psammead agreed that it would try to wish the Phoenix back home, though it could not understand why the children wanted this.

'It's all fire and feathers!' it told them.

It puffed itself up, but soon let out its breath in a long shuddering sigh.

'I'm out of practice,' it told them. 'I might try again later, when you've gone. Goodbye!'

It whirled itself back into the sand, and the children had to be content with that.

They were in the train on the way back home when Robert found a letter in his pocket. It was the one mother had given him to post several days ago, to tell Eliza which train to meet.

'That's torn it, Bobs!' Cyril told him. 'Now we'll have to spend our money on a cab!'

When they arrived back at the house it was all in darkness. Cyril banged at the door, but no one answered.

'Where is everyone?' Anthea wondered.

Then they heard the rattle and click of the letter box. Cyril lifted the flap and peered in and saw a golden eye.

'Phoenix!'

'Ssshh!' came the Phoenix's voice. 'Are you alone?'

'Yes, really,' said Anthea. 'And you don't know how glad we are that you're back, dear beautiful Phoenix!'

The latch was too stiff for the Phoenix's beak to lift, so it told them to go round the back, where the scullery window had been left open. Cyril scrambled through, then let the others in.

'But where are Eliza and Lily?' asked Anthea.

The Phoenix shook its head.

'They will sleep tonight at the house of a Mrs Wigson. She is giving a large party in honour of cook's late husband's cousin's sister-in-law's mother's ninetieth birthday.'

'Cheek!' said Robert.

'I don't think they ought to have gone off without leave,' said Anthea, 'however many relations they have, or however old they are.'

'Well, it's New Year's Eve, so I vote we have a jolly good feast!' said Cyril.

So they sat in the kitchen and ate everything from the pantry.

'Now what?' said Robert.

'The carpet! Let's see if it's back in the nursery!'

Cyril raced off, and came back grinning from ear to ear and with the carpet rolled under his arm.

'Now – where shall we go?'

'Nowhere,' said Anthea.

The others looked at her.

'You know we can't. It's after dark, and mother wouldn't like it.'

'But it's New Year's Eve!' said Robert. 'I want some fun.'

It was the Phoenix who came up with the answer.

'Send the carpet back to the land where it came from. Pin a note to it, wishing that it will bring back some of the most delightful products of its native land!'

Cyril wrote the note and pinned it to the carpet. At once it vanished, it dissolved into thin air. The children gasped.

'Just think!' said Jane. 'It does that with us *on* it! It makes me feel all funny!'

They went to the scullery to do the washing up while they waited for the carpet to return. When they went back to the kitchen they listened at the door. They could hear peculiar rustling and scrabbling sounds.

'It's alive, whatever it is!' whispered Jane.

'It could be a *tiger*!' said Anthea fearfully.

'It's no use sending the carpet to fetch precious things if you're afraid to look at them when they come,' the Phoenix told them.

Slowly, very slowly, Cyril opened the door. They stared and gasped.

'My hat!' said Robert.

'Oh, I've always wanted a cat!' cried Jane.

'*A* cat? My sainted aunt!'

The kitchen was filled with Persian cats, dozens and dozens of them. The floor was a sea of moving, mewing pussiness.

As soon as they saw the children the cats

began to mew so piteously that the Phoenix, made nervous by so many cats, flew up on to the mantelpiece.

'They might not know that I am the one and only Phoenix,' it said.

'What's the matter with the bounders?' demanded Cyril.

'Oh pussies, do be *quiet*!' Jane put her hands over her ears. 'We can't hear ourselves think!'

'I imagine they are hungry,' said the Phoenix.

'We'll pin another note to the carpet, and ask it to go and fetch food,' Cyril said.

He wrote the note and pinned it on. Again the carpet dissolved under their very eyes.

The cats kept up their horrible mewing and yowling. Outside, a policeman who was plodding past heard. He stopped, listened, then began to descend the steps to the basement.

The children all had their hands over their ears when the carpet reappeared. They gaped. It was piled high with plump, shining silver fish. The smell was terrible.

'Ugh! What a stink!' Cyril pinched his nose

and rushed out, and the rest piled after him. They banged the kitchen door.

'Now the kitchen will smell of fish for evermore!' said Jane.

'Hello there!' came a deep voice.

The children stiffened. The voice seemed to come from the scullery. They went nervously in and through the window saw the face of a policeman.

'What's all this row?' he demanded. 'I'm a-coming in!'

Eight

The Cats, the Cow, and the Burglar

T HE CHILDREN TRIED their hardest to stop the policeman from going into the kitchen. But he was determined to find out what was going on. He was just about to open the kitchen door when there came a blood-curdling screech from the street.

'Stop, thief! Help! Murder! Murder!'

'Quick!' yelled Robert. 'Someone's being murdered!'

Off the policeman went to investigate. A

few minutes later the Phoenix appeared through the open back door.

'It was *you!*' cried Jane. 'Oh clever old Phoenix!'

They decided the cats must be mewing because they were thirsty. So the carpet was sent off again with a note asking it to fetch milk.

'What a night we're having of it!' remarked the Phoenix. 'I am worn out. Goodnight.'

Off it went. No sooner had it gone than the carpet reappeared.

'Oh glory!' gasped Cyril.

'That's torn it!' said Robert.

On the carpet was a large Jersey cow. It gazed mildly about and let out a moo.

'Oh *now* what?' wailed Jane.

The children gazed helplessly at the cow, and it gazed mildly back. It let out another moo.

'We asked for it, I suppose,' said Cyril at last. 'We did ask for milk.'

'But how do we get it *out?*'

No one had ever milked a cow before, but

both the boys were willing to have a try. Anthea fetched a large enamel bowl and Robert knelt by the cow. The cow moved off to inspect the dresser, ploughing its way among yowling cats. Robert caught up with it, and soon found out that milking is not as easy as it looks. Not a single drop could he manage.

'Oh, let's go to bed and leave the beastly cats and the hateful cow!' said Jane.

'We can't send them away,' Cyril pointed out. 'We've already used today's wishes.'

In the end the boys decided to bundle the cats into baskets and pillowcases and such, and go and leave them on people's doorsteps, like orphan foundlings. While they were gone, Jane and Anthea fell asleep in the drawing room, but Jane was woken by a loud clatter.

A passing burglar had seen the open back door and come in to try his luck. When he opened the door of the kitchen and saw the swarming cats and the Jersey cow, he could not believe his eyes. He had been celebrating the New Year with a few drinks, and thought perhaps he had had one too many.

Jane crept down and found him there, talking to the cow. He said she reminded him of a cow he had once known called Daisy.

'Mr Burglar . . .' Jane began timidly.

He turned and saw her.

'Are you real, miss?' he asked. 'Or something I'll wake up from presently?'

'I'm quite real,' she told him. 'And so are they. Don't worry, I shan't send for the police. Do you know how to milk a cow?'

He did. He sat down, and had already filled the bucket with milk when the boys arrived back. The noise had woken Anthea, and she came down too. They all fetched bowls and saucers, and soon the thirsty cats were licking and lapping.

'Mr Burglar, how did you know the house would be empty?' Jane asked.

'Except for us,' added Robert.

The burglar had heard Eliza talking in the market. She said that the master and mistress were away, so she and Lily were going to a party at Mrs Wigson's, and would stay all night.

'They'll be back in the morning though,' said Cyril glumly. 'And there are plenty of cats still left. I suppose *you* wouldn't like them?'

'Persian cats are very valuable,' Robert told the burglar. 'Father says they're worth pounds and pounds.'

It turned out that the burglar had a mate who had a barrow. As soon as he had finished milking, he went to fetch him. The pair bundled up the cats and loaded them on to the barrow.

'I shouldn't like to get caught by the coppers with this little lot,' the burglar said. 'What kind of story would I tell them?'

Just then all the bells began to ring. It was midnight, and the New Year had begun.

'Now we can have another wish!' said Cyril. 'Get rid of the cow!'

So they sent the carpet off with the cow and went to bed.

*

Next morning the kitchen was still littered with fishbones.

'We'll clear them up,' said Cyril, 'but we're not letting Eliza and Lily off. They shouldn't have gone out without asking leave.'

'In fact, they deserve a booby trap,' said Robert, and the others agreed.

Eliza and cook had a real fright when they pushed open the kitchen door and the pail of water tipped over them. They were dripping wet when the children came out from their hiding places. Eliza started to scold them.

'Don't you begin jawing us!' Cyril told her. 'We know too much! How was Mrs Wigson's party?'

'We could tell mother,' added Jane.

'And we'll have treacle roly-poly and tinned tongue for dinner, thank you very much!' said Robert.

From now on there was no more mutton stew and semolina for dinner. Eliza and cook could not for the life of them think how the children had found out they were at Mrs Wigson's. Lily thought that perhaps they had a crystal ball. Nor could they make out why there was such a horrible smell of fish in the kitchen.

'And everything covered in 'airs,' said Eliza. 'Look like cat 'airs. Can't be. They 'aven't got a cat.'

They both agreed that something rum had been going on while they were out. But they could never ever have guessed at the truth.

Nine
Prison

W HEN THE CHILDREN went up to the nursery they found the Phoenix gazing sadly down at the carpet.

'What's up, old bird?' asked Robert.

'That is,' and it pointed a claw at the carpet. 'Look at the bare, worn patches, and that dreadful tear.'

'It does look a dog's dinner, rather,' agreed Cyril.

'That carpet has been your good and faithful servant,' said the Phoenix sternly. 'And how have you repaid it?'

'We'll mend it,' Anthea said. 'I'll get my sewing box.'

The girls began to darn.

'I don't see why you can't help!' Jane told the boys. She hated sewing.

'They can go and fetch some more wool,' said Anthea. 'We shan't have nearly enough.'

'Good idea!' said Cyril. 'Work up an appetite for dinner!'

'Tinned tongue and treacle roly.' Robert smacked his lips.

The boys were just coming out of the wool shop when they saw an excited crowd of people and two policemen. They hurried over and saw that in the midst of the crowd was their burglar, with his barrow-load of cats.

'Oh no!' Robert groaned. 'He's been nabbed!'

The poor burglar was trying to explain how he had come by the cats.

'I got 'em in exchange for milking a cow. In a basement kitchen it was, up Camden Town way.'

The crowd roared with laughter.

'Perhaps you can give us the name and address of this cow, sir?' said one policeman.

'They 'adn't got a flock of sheep in there as well, by any chance?' asked the other.

'Shall we go forward?' Robert whispered.

Cyril shook his head.

'They'd never believe us. Any more than they believe him. Come on – let's tell the girls.'

Anthea and Jane were still busy stitching the carpet, and being lectured by the Phoenix. In the olden days, it told them, the carpet had never lain on the floor to be trodden on by careless boots. It had hung in splendour on the wall.

'It belonged to kings and sultans,' it said. 'And when wishes were required, people always took their shoes off. I suggest – oops!'

It flew to the fender in alarm as the door burst open.

'I say, you'll never believe it!' cried Cyril.

'They've got him! The coppers!'

Of course, all the children felt dreadfully guilty. Their burglar had done them a good turn, and now he was going to prison because of it. They sat about planning his rescue. Jane had the best idea.

'Send him to the sunny southern shore!'

'Of course! Then he'll have cook for company!'

They had already used one of today's wishes, sending back the cow. They decided not to risk going to the island themselves.

'We'll go tomorrow, to see how he's getting on.'

After dinner, Eliza and Lily had a nap. As soon as they were asleep the children crowded on to the carpet.

Cyril made the wish, and instantly the giddy-go-round-and-falling-lift swept over them. When they opened their eyes they were in a small whitewashed cell. On a narrow bed under the grilled window lay their burglar, snoring gently.

'Blow!' whispered Cyril. 'Now we'll have to wake him.'

Jane tiptoed over and touched him gently. He jerked up and let out a yelp. There was the sound of heavy boots and a jangling of keys in the passage outside. The children ducked down.

''Ere, you, stop that rowing!' came a voice. The burglar blinked and shook his head.

'Right you are, guv!' he shouted. 'I was only talking in my sleep! No offence!'

Then the boots began to tread heavily away. The burglar stared and scratched his head.

''Ow the blue Moses did you get in?' he asked hoarsely.

'On the carpet,' Jane told him, and pointed.

'We've come to save you,' said Anthea. 'Listen – where would you like to go in the whole world?'

'Where?' said the burglar. 'Anywhere, after this!'

'How about a sunny southern shore?' asked Robert.

'Oh *yes*, and 'ow about the moon!'

'We can send you there, whether you believe us or not,' Cyril told him. He knelt and pinned a note on the carpet. He had written it earlier. It said: 'Please take our burglar to the sunny southern shore and then come straight back here and take us home.'

'What's that there?' asked the burglar suspiciously.

'It's – like a postage stamp!' said Robert.

'Yes! We're posting you there!' said Jane. 'Now – stand on the carpet.'

He shook his head and stepped forward. Next minute he had vanished. The children stood silent for a moment, looking at each other.

'Don't worry, Pusscat,' Anthea told Jane. 'We'll go and see him tomorrow, when Eliza and cook are out shopping.'

'*If* we get out,' said Robert. 'If we're still not stuck here in prison!'

Jane let out a little shriek, but had no sooner done so than the carpet reappeared. It didn't seem to take much notice of time. The children thankfully clambered on, and next minute were safely back in the nursery.

When the burglar awoke the next day he still could not believe his luck.

'I dunno . . .' he muttered. 'Cats, cows, kids on carpets with postage stamps . . . and now this . . . it's a blooming mystery.'

He wandered along through the tropical flowers, sucking at a peach. He found himself on a wide beach, and before him was an amazing sight. Cook was sitting and singing, crowned with flowers and surrounded by attendants. The burglar stared and rubbed his eyes.

Then cook saw him.

'Oooh!' she said. 'A nice young feller! Another dream, if I'm not mistook!'

She smiled at the burglar and he smiled back.

'Come alone!' she called. 'There's no need to be shy! I may be queen, but I ain't stuck up, I 'ope!'

So he came, and the nearer he got, the more he liked what he saw.

'This here's only a dream what you've come into,' cook told him.

'Then it's a blooming good one!' he told her, and bowed gallantly.

Cook blushed mightily.

Near by, the carpet suddenly appeared, with the children. Cook and the burglar were too busy gazing into one another's eyes to notice. When at last they did see the children they were not in the least surprised. To them it was just another part of the dream. And by now they were getting on so well that the burglar asked cook to marry him.

'A wedding! Hurray!' cried Jane and Anthea.

But there was a snag. Cook wanted to be married properly, by a proper clergyman. So that was the end of that – or seemed to be.

Then Anthea had a wonderful idea . . .

Ten

The Burglar's Bride

THE REVEREND SEPTIMUS Blenkinsop was in his study reading. Above him a large marble clock ticked heavily. Then there came another sound, a kind of soft shushing. He raised his head, and as he did so, a carpet appeared right under his eyes.

He blinked and stared. He took off his glasses and stared. He put them on again and stared.

'Why, bless my soul!' he exclaimed.

Outside the door his sister Amelia called,

'Tea, Septimus dear! Come along, or it will be getting cold!'

'Coming, Amelia!' he called.

He got up and went over to the carpet. Then, to test whether it was really there, he stepped on to it. Next minute he was caught in the tipsy-topsy-turvy feeling of the magic, and he was on a South Sea island. At least, he was *half* there. He had stepped on one of Jane's darns, so the magic was only half working. He could see white sands and palm trees, but he could also see his own study and hear the tick of his marble clock.

'It's him! It's the Reverend Blenkinsop!' he heard Anthea's voice say.

'He's only half there!' said Cyril.

The children were having exactly the same trouble. The clergyman was there, all right, but they could see through him as if he were a ghost.

'It must be a dream, of course . . .' murmured Septimus.

'Has he gone off his chump, do you think?' came Robert's voice.

'Must be the bottled gooseberries we had for dinner . . .' As he spoke, the Reverend Septimus Blenkinsop stepped off the carpet, and at once he was there, really there.

The children cheered and the burglar squeezed cook's hand. Now they could get married.

It was a wonderful wedding. The children danced and sang with the rest, and ate lots of delicious food at the feast. Septimus enjoyed it too. He thought he was having the most amazing dream of his whole life.

At last it was time to go. The children and Septimus got on to the carpet and waved goodbye to the happy pair. First the carpet returned to Septimus's study. Then, as soon as he had stepped off, it vanished again to take the children home.

He stood blinking and looking about him. It was all there, safe and solid – his desk, and chair and the ticking marble clock. Outside the door he could hear his sisters' voices.

'Are you *sure* he answered when you called him to tea?' asked Selina.

'Selina, I shall not repeat this again. He answered. He said, "I'm coming!", just as he always does.'

'Very well,' said Selina. 'We will make one last search, then call the police!'

The Reverend Septimus Blenkinsop was not really listening. He leaned forward and touched his marble clock – just to make sure it was really there.

'Real . . . quite real . . .' he murmured.

Then in burst Selina and Amelia. They didn't believe *their* eyes, either. If they had looked in the study once they had looked twenty times. And now here was their brother, cool as a cucumber, looking as if he had been there all the time. There was some explaining to do . . .

The next day a letter arrived. It was Jane's turn to open it.

'Hurray, hurray! Mother comes home today!'

Anthea took the letter. 'Not till nearly bed-time, though.'

They were all thinking the same thing. Once mother was home there would be much less chance to go for exciting trips on the carpet. It was, in any case, as they had to admit, now very threadbare.

'We could have one last carpet trip today,' said Robert. He still hankered after America.

'I want to get a really nice present for mother,' Jane said.

'And where would we get the money?' asked Robert.

'I'll tell you what,' said Cyril. 'Suppose we wish the carpet to take us somewhere where we could find a purse with money in it.'

He got up, and as he did so caught his boot in one of the carpet's darns. There was a horrid tearing sound.

'Well, now you've done it!' his brother told him.

'Don't worry, Squirrel, I'll mend it,' Anthea said.

But there was no time. There were all kinds of things to arrange to celebrate the home-coming of mother and the Lamb.

The girls went down to the kitchen to ask cook to make a special cake with candles.

'First I've 'eard of cakes with candles and it's nobody's birthday!' said Lily after they had gone.

'Ooh, they're like that at this 'ouse,' Eliza told her.

The Phoenix decided that as it might be their last adventure, it would go along too. It made sure the children removed their boots before getting on to the carpet.

'But we'll need them when we get wherever we're going,' said Cyril. So they arranged them on the carpet in a little pile.

'Let's wish for the carpet to take us slowly this time,' Jane said. 'So's we can see where we're going.'

The children thought it best not to wish to find a purse, because if they did, they should take it straight to the police. They worked out a very carefully worded wish. Once they were on the carpet, Anthea made it.

'We wish to go somewhere where we can get a sovereign for mother's present, and get it in some way that she'll believe in, and not think wrong.'

'That is rather a long wish,' observed the Phoenix.

'Oh – and do please go slowly, dear carpet,' Anthea added.

And so it did. After the first dizziness, they found themselves sailing over the roofs of Camden Town. The carpet wove its way between the chimneypots. Although it was flying quite low, the children felt odd and giddy. They guessed that this was because of the worn patches.

'Where's it taking us?' Robert wondered. He craned over to see. 'Look, there's the river, and – oooops!'

'Look out – the boots!' yelled Cyril.

One (Robert's) had already dropped through a tear in the carpet. Down it fell – smack next to Selina Blenkinsop in her garden below.

'Quick!' Jane lunged to rescue the other boots and so did Robert. Next minute they both disappeared through the hole in the carpet.

'Help!' screamed Anthea.

Jane and Robert landed with a thud on a rooftop. Anthea and Cyril peered anxiously over the edge of the carpet.

'Are you hurt?' called Cyril.

'Oh – get us off, can't you!' called Jane.

But the carpet went sailing on, and the voices of their brother and sister grew fainter.

'You can't wish to go back,' the Phoenix told them. 'The carpet has not fulfilled your first wish yet.'

'But how will they get down?' cried Anthea.

'They'll yell till someone gets them down,' Cyril told her. 'Then they can tram it home.'

'What – without their boots? Oh!'

The carpet was dropping. Below lay what looked like a perfectly ordinary street.

'What's it bringing us here for?' Cyril wondered.

'I expect it knows,' Anthea told him. 'It usually does.'

And it did. The first person to come along, once the children had landed and hidden the Phoenix and the carpet, was Uncle Felix. On his arm was pretty Miss Peasmarsh. They were off for a jaunt on the river, he told them. He must have been in a very good mood (or keen to get rid of the children), because he slipped a coin into Cyril's hand and carried jauntily on his way.

Anthea and Cyril stared at the golden coin that lay in his palm. It was exactly what they had wished for – a sovereign.

'Good old carpet!' said Cyril.

'Excuse *me*!' came a muffled voice near by.

'Good old carpet *and* Phoenix!' said Anthea hastily.

They went home and waited for Robert and Jane. But as time passed and there was still no sign of them, the Phoenix grew fidgety.

'I can bear it no longer!' it said. 'My Robert – who set my egg in the fire!'

And it flew off out of the window.

Meanwhile, Robert and Jane were certainly not catching a tram home. When they first landed on the roof they did exactly what Cyril had said they would do. They yelled down to passers-by to attract attention. But no one so much as glanced up.

Jane began to cry. Robert began to look for other ways of escaping. Soon he found one – a skylight that had been left unlocked.

'Quick – here!' he called.

Between them they raised the heavy skylight, but as they did so it fell back on to the tiles.

Crash!

From the attic below came a bloodcurdling shriek. Next minute the children were looking down into the horrified eyes of Miss Amelia Blenkinsop!

She opened her mouth wide to let out another scream.

'Oh don't, please don't!' cried Jane. 'We won't hurt you!'

'Where – where are the rest of your gang?' quavered Amelia.

'The others have gone on, on the magic carpet,' Jane said.

'Shut up, idiot!' Robert hissed. 'Oh crikey – that's torn it!'

Eleven

The Beginning of
the End

AMELIA GOT TO her feet, then backed towards the door. She never once took her eyes off the children. Once outside, they could hear her calling as she went downstairs, 'Septimus! Quickly! Selina!'

'Quick!' said Robert. 'Now!'

He scrambled into the opening, hung by his hands, then dropped.

'Now you,' he said. 'Just shut your eyes if you're scared!'

Jane dropped beside him and they made for the door. But they could hear footsteps and voices. They hastily hid behind a pile of boxes.

The ladies came hurrying in and looked up at the skylight.

'Gone! They've gone!' shrieked Amelia.

'Perhaps you imagined them, dear,' said Selina.

'And perhaps *you* imagined boots falling from the sky!' snapped Amelia. 'They must be up there on the roof. Help me!'

They dragged a large box underneath the skylight and then climbed on to it, clutching their skirts. The children saw their chance and ran. But they had only reached the second landing when they saw a maid with a coal scuttle coming up the stairs. Robert spotted an open door. He nipped inside, followed by Jane. Long curtains hung at the windows. They had only just managed to hide behind them when the maid came in. She left the scuttle in the hearth and went out.

'Shall we run for it?' Jane whispered.

'No – wait! Listen!'

Amelia hurried in.

'Septimus?' She looked around. 'He's never vanished again!'

'Look! Oh look! The missionary box!' shrieked Selina.

She was pointing at a large collecting box. The label was torn and the box was open and empty.

'I knew it!' cried Amelia. 'Selina – it was a gang! They sent the children in to distract us, while the rest of the gang robbed the house!'

'Amelia, we must call the police from the window. I'll – eeeech!'

It was hard to tell who had the bigger fright – the sisters or the children. Jane and Robert were well and truly caught.

But had they known it, help was on its way. The Phoenix had flown to the sandpit, to ask the Psammead a favour. When it got there, the Psammead was sitting in a pile of sand, looking exceedingly cross and frowsty.

'Oh, *you* again!' it said rudely. 'I suppose

91

those silly children have got themselves into some kind of bother!'

'Two of them are stuck among some chimneypots in Deptford,' the Phoenix told it.

The Psammead sniffed.

'You don't surprise me,' it said. 'And I suppose you want me to get them down. What a pity *you* cannot grant wishes! You are nothing more than a glorified egg!'

It was in no great hurry to grant the wish. Meantime, Robert and Jane were struggling to free themselves.

'We *aren't* burglars!'

'We never touched the beastly missionary box!'

The door opened and in came the Reverend Septimus Blenkinsop. The children let out such shrieks of joy that the two ladies jumped and let go of them.

'It's our own clergyman!'

'You married the burglar for us!' added Robert.

'Burglar!' moaned Selina, and sat down suddenly.

Everyone started trying to explain at once. Poor Septimus could hardly hear a word anyone said, but at last managed to get his own word in.

'*I* opened the missionary box.'

'There!' cried Jane triumphantly.

'We *told* you!'

And then they vanished. They simply melted into thin air. The Blenkinsops stared blankly, speechless. They closed their eyes, then opened them again. Magic was too much for them.

Thanks to the Phoenix and the Psammead, Robert and Jane were wished back home. Cyril showed them the golden sovereign, and they rushed out to buy presents for mother and the Lamb. Later that day there was a welcome-home party, with cake and candles and surprises galore.

Next morning the children had to send the carpet off with a note: 'Please fetch Robert's boot in double quick time.' And so it did.

Then, later that day, a telegram arrived from father, to say that he would be home next day, and he had arranged a special treat for the children. They were to go to the Garrick Theatre, all on their own, to see *The Water Babies*.

It seemed ages to wait, and the children were dressed in their best bibs and tuckers long before it was time to go. As Anthea arranged her hair in the glass for the twentieth time, she noticed the Phoenix perched on the fender. It seemed to be drooping.

'Don't you feel well, Phoenix dear?' she asked.

'I am not sick,' it replied, 'but I am getting old.'

'But you've hardly been hatched any time at all!' said Jane.

'I am old,' it repeated. 'I am weary. I feel as if I ought to lay my egg and lay me down to my fiery sleep.'

The children hated it to talk like this. Already the carpet was threadbare, and now it looked as if they might lose the Phoenix, too.

'Come to the theatre with us!' said Jane.

Robert had to keep it hidden under his jacket on the way to the theatre. Father had arranged for them to have a box of their own, with little gilt chairs and velvet drapes. Mother and father went off to have supper.

'And remember – wait here for us when the show's over,' father said. 'Don't go down. There'll be crush, and we'd never find you.'

The Phoenix perked up no end when Robert let it out and it saw where it was.

'Tell me, is this my temple?' it asked. And, as the house lights went down, 'Oh, the sun is setting!'

The curtain went up, and from then on there was no stopping the Phoenix. It thought the actors on the stage were there in its honour, and kept demanding why there was no fire, in a very loud voice. The audience made shushing noises and glared up at the box. At the end of the first act an attendant came to ask the children to keep their bird quiet.

But when the curtain rose for the second act the Phoenix really took off. It launched itself from the balcony and began to fly round and round, sweeping in great circles and crying, 'Fire! Fire! Why is there no fire?'

To the children's horror, they saw that sparks were glowing where the Phoenix had passed, and they were fanned by its wings into little buds of flame. Smoke wreaths began to curl upwards.

'Fire! Fire!' The word ran through the audience. Some people got to their feet, shouting, and the curtain came down. There was pandemonium as everyone tried to get out at once.

'Oh, what shall we do, what shall we do?' cried Jane.

'Stay here,' said Cyril firmly. 'Father told us to. And I've read about fires and think we'll be safe.'

'Where's that bird?' Robert scanned about through the smoke and flames, but there was no sign of the Phoenix.

'It's gone!'

'Oh, I wish we'd never *met* the beastly bird!' screamed Jane.

'The Phoenix has never ratted on us yet,'

said Robert. 'It'll see us through somehow. I believe in the Phoenix!'

And at that very moment the Phoenix was there – and the carpet!

'Oh thank heaven!' sobbed Anthea. And the children scrambled on to it as quickly as they could, taking care to avoid the darns.

'I can't understand all this fuss over a little fire!' said the Phoenix.

Next minute they were safely back in the nursery. They stared at one another. They all had faces grimed and smirched with smoke.

'Oh – mother and father!' gasped Anthea. 'How awful! They'll think we've been burned to cinders!'

Twelve
The End of the End

JUST THEN THE children heard their mother's voice below.

'Children! Children! Are you there?'

There were tears and hugs and an amazing tale to tell. Father said that he and mother had rushed straight to the Garrick when they heard it was on fire. And then the strangest thing had happened. A bird, he said, a huge yellow pigeon, had perched on his shoulder, and recited the names of the four children in his ear. It had then perched on the other shoulder and done exactly the same.

'Er – wasn't it more like an eagle?' Cyril asked.

'It wasn't a pigeon, it was a big orange-coloured cockatoo!' said mother.

Of course, the children knew that it was neither a pigeon nor a cockatoo, and were grateful to the Phoenix. All the same, it had behaved very badly. A theatre had burned down and their poor mother was terribly shocked. They had a stern word with the Phoenix when they went back up. At first it was sulky. It had enjoyed the evening hugely.

Luckily, it turned out that the Phoenix could undo fires, as well as start them. Cyril said that was what it had jolly well better do. So the Phoenix flew off into the night to set the theatre to rights again.

'It was a night to remember!' it said as it went. 'I shall treasure its memory for ever!'

Next morning mother was still so badly

shaken that she had to stay in bed. The children felt horribly guilty, but they knew in their hearts that it was not their fault. Each thought, but hardly liked to say out loud, that it was time for the Phoenix to go.

Even once they had admitted it, they did not see how they could tell the Phoenix so without hurting its feelings dreadfully. As it happened, they need not have worried.

Later that day the Phoenix perched on the fender, looked round at the children, and said, 'Weep not. I really beg that you will not weep. The time has come when I must leave you.'

They all let out deep sighs of relief.

'Do not sigh,' it told them. 'Give me what is left of the carpet and let me go.'

The children left the Phoenix alone with the carpet, and went off in search of scented woods and spices to make a ritual fire. They were very quiet. They knew that the Phoenix and the carpet must go, but now that the time had come could hardly bear it. Magic would disappear, and their lives would be dull and ordinary again.

When they returned to the nursery they tapped on the door.

'Enter!' came the voice of the Phoenix.

They went in. Their eyes went straight to the carpet, and they gasped in wonder. Lying there was a beautiful egg of palest gold – exactly like the one that had tumbled out so many weeks ago. The Phoenix sat near by, clucking with pride and joy.

'Oh you clever thing!' said Jane.

'As fine an egg as ever I laid in all my born days!' said the Phoenix proudly.

'It's spot on!' said Cyril. 'A beauty!'

'Look – we've got all the things for the funeral pyre,' said Robert.

'Oh don't say funeral!' begged Jane.

First, Robert wrote a note to pin to the carpet. The Phoenix told him what to write: 'Please – there is no harm in politeness – take this beautiful, precious, sacred egg somewhere safe, where it will not be hatched for another two thousand years.'

'I can't believe it!' said Anthea. 'Two thousand years!'

'*We* shan't be here to see it, that is for certain,' said Cyril.

Robert knelt and pinned the note to the carpet. Under their very eyes it rolled itself up round the egg – and vanished.

There was a long silence. There was no going back now.

'That's that, then,' said Robert flatly.

'Bear up,' the Phoenix told him. 'What do you think *I* don't suffer, being parted from my precious new-laid egg like this? Come, build my fire. My hour has come.'

Cyril went to the fire and started putting on the sandalwood pencils, the spices and oils. Anthea helped him, tears running down her face.

Robert touched the Phoenix's soft head.

'Oh I can't bear to let you go!'

The Phoenix rubbed its beak softly against Robert's ear.

'Farewell, Robert of my heart! I have loved you well.'

'Oh we've loved *you*!' burst out Jane. The tears were dripping from her cheeks.

Now the fire was fizzing, with little blue and green flames among the orange.

'Oh I can't bear it!' sobbed Anthea.

The Phoenix spoke in a hollow, faraway voice: 'Farewell . . . farewell . . . farewell . . . farewell . . .'

It fluttered up and circled the room one last time on wide gold wings.

'Oh goodbye! Goodbye!' cried the children.

The Phoenix flew down and settled in the soft heart of the fire. The spices fizzed and the flames flickered and flared about it. It did not burn. It seemed to grow red hot right to its core. It turned from gold to red.

The children gazed through their tears. They gazed as if by doing so they could bring the Phoenix back, even now.

Then, softly, it fell into a heap of white ashes and was swallowed by the flames.

The children were fixed like statues, still gazing into the fire. Then, faint and far away, they seemed to hear an echoey rustle of flying wings. They looked up eagerly, half expecting to see the Phoenix.

Drifting, floating, swirled a single golden feather. It fluttered to the hearth, and Robert picked it up.